Dear Parent:

Congratulations! Your child is taking the first steps on an exciting journey. The destination? Independent reading!

STEP INTO READING® will help your child get there. The program offers five steps to reading success. Each step includes fun stories and colorful art. There are also Step into Reading Sticker Books, Step into Reading Math Readers, Step into Reading Write-In Readers, Step into Reading Phonics Readers, and Step into Reading Phonics First Steps! Boxed Sets—a complete literacy program with something for every child.

Learning to Read, Step by Step!

Ready to Read   Preschool–Kindergarten
• big type and easy words • rhyme and rhythm • picture clues
For children who know the alphabet and are eager to begin reading.

Reading with Help   Preschool–Grade 1
• basic vocabulary • short sentences • simple stories
For children who recognize familiar words and sound out new words with help.

Reading on Your Own   Grades 1–3
• engaging characters • easy-to-follow plots • popular topics
For children who are ready to read on their own.

Reading Paragraphs   Grades 2–3
• challenging vocabulary • short paragraphs • exciting stories
For newly independent readers who read simple sentences with confidence.

Ready for Chapters   Grades 2–4
• chapters • longer paragraphs • full-color art
For children who want to take the plunge into chapter books but still like colorful pictures.

STEP INTO READING® is designed to give every child a successful reading experience. The grade levels are only guides. Children can progress through the steps at their own speed, developing confidence in their reading, no matter what their grade.

Remember, a lifetime love of reading starts with a single step!

For Ava, Audrey, and Lilly—my little buddies
—M.L.

Copyright © 2009 Disney Enterprises, Inc./Pixar. All rights reserved. Original *Toy Story* elements © Disney Enterprises, Inc. Slinky® Dog is a registered trademark of Poof-Slinky, Inc. © Poof-Slinky, Inc. Etch A Sketch® © The Ohio Art Company. Published in the United States by Random House Children's Books, a division of Random House, Inc., 1745 Broadway, New York, NY 10019, and in Canada by Random House of Canada Limited, Toronto, in conjunction with Disney Enterprises, Inc.

Step into Reading, Random House, and the Random House colophon are registered trademarks of Random House, Inc.

Visit us on the Web!
www.stepintoreading.com
www.randomhouse.com/kids

Educators and librarians, for a variety of teaching tools, visit us at
www.randomhouse.com/teachers

Library of Congress Cataloging-in-Publication Data
Lagonegro, Melissa.
Friends forever / by Melissa Lagonegro ; [illustrated by Studio Iboix and the Disney Storybook Artists]. — 1st ed.
    p. cm. — (Step into reading. Step 2 book)
ISBN 978-0-7364-2597-1 (trade) — ISBN 978-0-7364-8069-7 (lib. bdg.)
I. Disney Storybook Artists. II. Toy story (Motion picture).
III. Title.
PZ7.L14317Fr 2009   [E]—dc22   2008053160

Printed in the United States of America   10 9 8 7 6 5 4 3 2 1

Disney · PIXAR

TOY STORY

FRIENDS FOREVER

By Melissa Lagonegro
Illustrated by Studio Iboix
and the Disney Storybook Artists

Random House 🏠 New York

Buzz and Woody are
Andy's favorite toys.
They are
best friends.

Oh, no!
Woody has been stolen!

Woody is trapped.
He meets Jessie,
Bullseye, and
the Prospector.

They are
the Roundup gang.
Woody is a member of
the Roundup gang, too!

Buzz wants
to save Woody.
Andy's other toys help.

Woody learns about
the Roundup gang.
He makes friends.
He has fun.

Buzz looks for Woody.

Andy's other toys help.

Woody misses Andy.
But he will not leave
his new friends.
He is worried about them.

Buzz finds Woody!

He wants Woody

to come home.

So do the other toys.

Woody asks
the Roundup gang
to come home
with him!
But the Prospector
blocks their way.

He will not let
the others leave.
He is not their friend
after all.

Woody and
the Roundup gang
are in trouble.

The man is taking them
far away.
Buzz and Slinky
try to help.

The toys go after Woody!
Buzz drives a truck.

Buzz has a plan
to save Woody.
The toys follow Woody.
They go to the airport.

Buzz races
to the rescue!

Oh, no!
Jessie is trapped
in the case.
She is put
on a plane!

Woody tries
to help Jessie.
They are in danger!

Buzz and Bullseye save Jessie and Woody!

The toys go
home to Andy.
They will all be
friends forever.